Oh, Tucker!

Steven Kroll

illustrated by

Scott Nash

WALKER BOOKS

AND SUBSIDIARIES

LONDON • BOSTON • SYDNEY

ER!

Time for breakfast!"
Tina called.

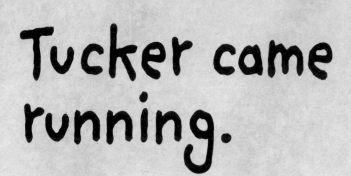

Tucker came running.

WHAM!
He knocked over a dustbin.

He jumped up and licked Tina's chin.
"Oh, Tucker!" Tina giggled.

Tucker pushed open the front door and raced into the house.

WHAM!

He knocked over a vase of flowers.

WHAM!

He knocked a china plate on to the floor.

"Oh, Tucker!" Tina groaned.

Tucker ran for the stairs.
"Tucker, no!" Tina cried.
"It's breakfast-time!"

But Tucker didn't listen.
He had to say good morning
to Tina's parents.
He bounded up the stairs.

Mum and Dad were fast asleep.
Tucker didn't mind.
WHAM!
He landed on the bed.

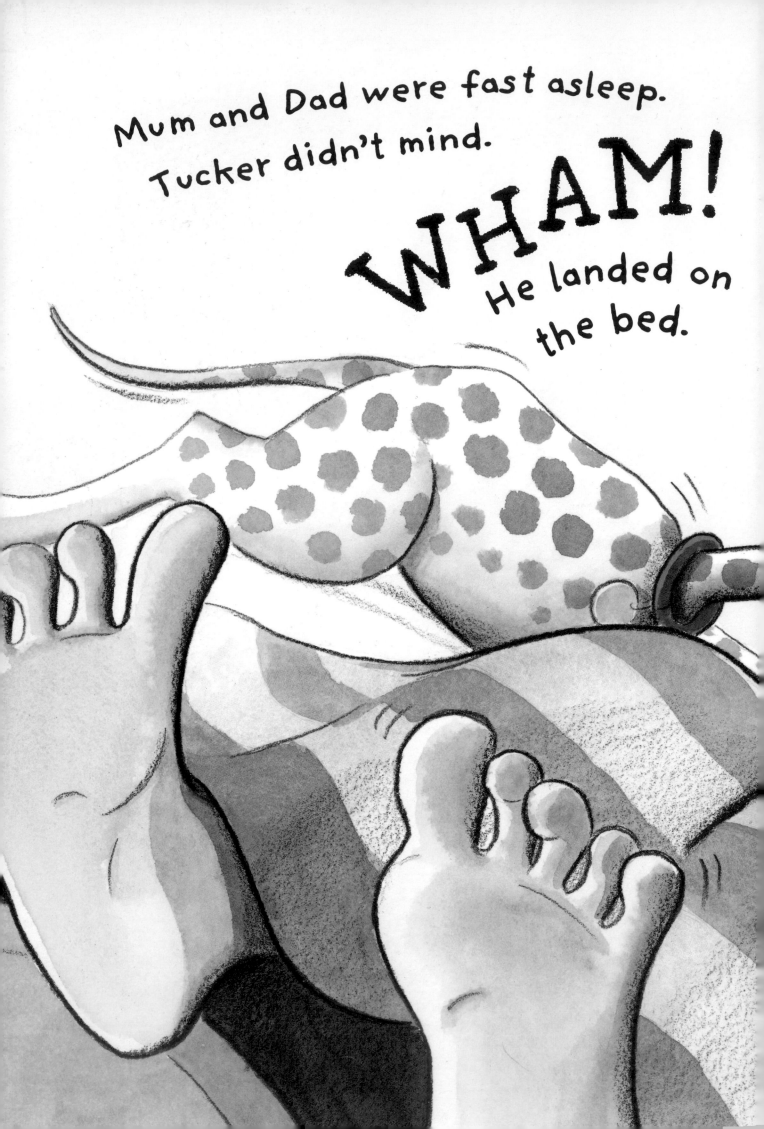

Tucker licked their faces and wagged his tail. **WHAM!** He knocked over the bedside lamp.

Tucker barked,
he ran back to the stairs –

and slipped!

He scrambled to his feet.

WHAM!

He knocked over a table and a lamp.

The lampshade plopped on his head.

Tucker couldn't see but that didn't stop him. He zigzagged through the living room.

"Oh, Tucker, WAIT!" Tina cried.

But Tucker didn't listen.

WHAM!
He knocked over a chair.
WHAM!
He knocked over a vase.

WHAM! He knocked over a plant and a bowl and a china cat.

WHAM! WHAM! WHAM!

Tucker stepped on Tina's
skateboard and zoomed down
the hall! Tina hid her eyes.

"Oh, Tucker!"

HAM!

He crashed against the kitchen sink.
The lampshade flew off his head.

Tina hurried in. Mum and Dad
hurried in, too.

"Here, Tucker, look," Tina said.
She set his dish down in front of him.
They all held their breath.

Tucker dug in.
"Finally," said Tina.
Mum and Dad sighed with relief.

Tina smiled.
Such a nice dog. Such a friendly dog.
Who could possibly scold him?

"Oh, Tucker!"